The Mermaid and the Shoe

For Billie

Text and illustrations © 2014 K. G. Campbell

All rights reserved. No part of this publication may be reproduced, stored
in a retrieval system or transmitted, in any form or by any means, without the
prior written permission of Kids Can Press Ltd. or, in case of photocopying
or other reprographic copying, a license from The Canadian Copyright
Licensing Agency (Access Copyright). For an Access Copyright license,
visit www.accesscopyright.ca or call toll free to 1-800-893-5777.

Kids Can Press acknowledges the financial support of the Government of Ontario,
through the Ontario Media Development Corporation's Ontario Book Initiative.

Published in Canada by   Published in the U.S. by
Kids Can Press Ltd.   Kids Can Press Ltd.
25 Dockside Drive   2250 Military Road
Toronto, ON M5A 0B5   Tonawanda, NY 14150

www.kidscanpress.com

The artwork in this book was rendered in watercolor and pencil crayon.
The text is set in Fairfield Light and Bookeyed Suzanne.

Acquired by Tara Walker. Edited by Yvette Ghione.
Designed by Karen Powers

This book is smyth sewn casebound.
Manufactured in Shenzhen, China, in 1/2016, by Asia Pacific Offset

CM 14 0 9 8 7 6 5 4

Library and Archives Canada Cataloguing in Publication

Campbell, K. G., author, illustrator

The mermaid and the shoe / written and illustrated by K. G. Campbell.

ISBN 978-1-55453-771-6 (bound)

I. Title.

PZ7.C15512Mer 2014   j813´.6   C2013-905378-6

The Mermaid and the Shoe

Written and illustrated by

K. G. Campbell

KIDS CAN PRESS

King Neptune had fifty daughters.
Some might call them mermaids.

They were his pride and joy.

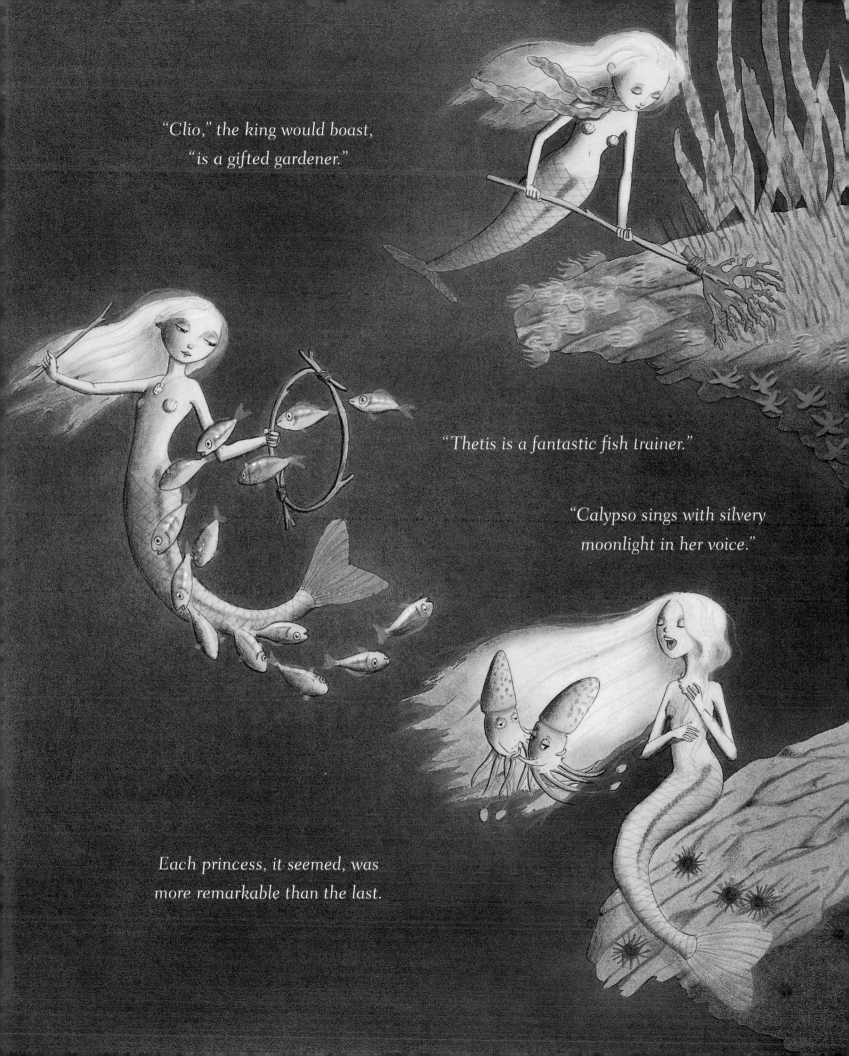

"Clio," the king would boast,
"is a gifted gardener."

"Thetis is a fantastic fish trainer."

"Calypso sings with silvery
moonlight in her voice."

Each princess, it seemed, was
more remarkable than the last.

Except Minnow.

Minnow's garden was
limp and sparse.

Fish did not follow
her instructions.

In her voice, there was
no light of any kind.

She did, however, ask
many, *many* questions.

"Why," she asked Clio,
"don't crabs have fins?"

"Where," she asked Thetis,
"do bubbles go?"

"What," she asked Calypso,
"lies beyond the kingdom?"

"Stop asking useless questions," Calypso replied,
"and be remarkable. Like the rest of us.
What are you even here for?"
Minnow wasn't sure.
"Useless!" hissed Calypso (for sisters can be mean that way).

And quietly, Minnow slipped away to float alone
where the current was warm and pleasant.

There, one day, something new drifted into Minnow's life.
She couldn't imagine what it was for,
but it was the loveliest thing she'd ever seen.

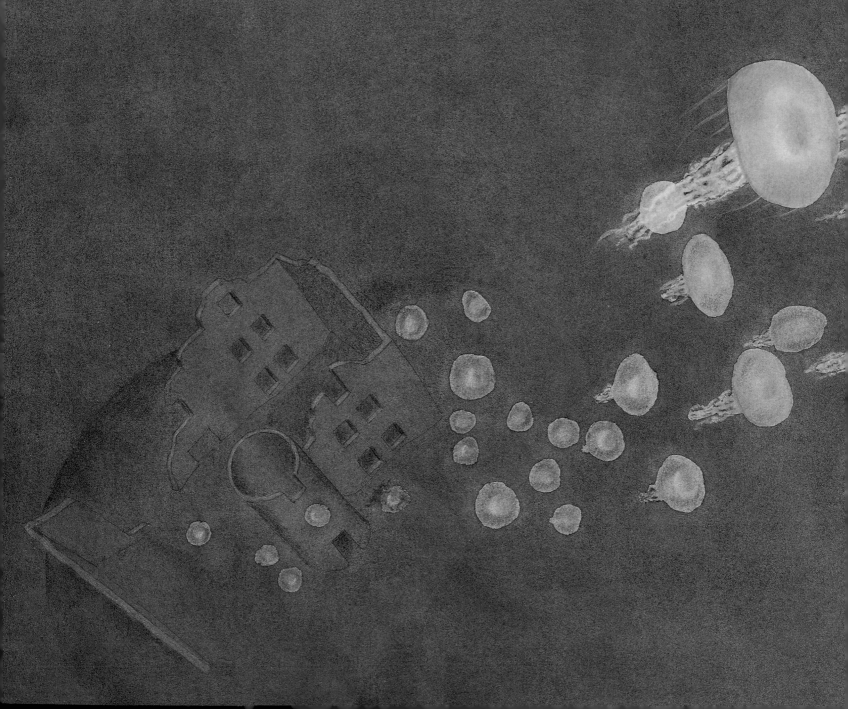

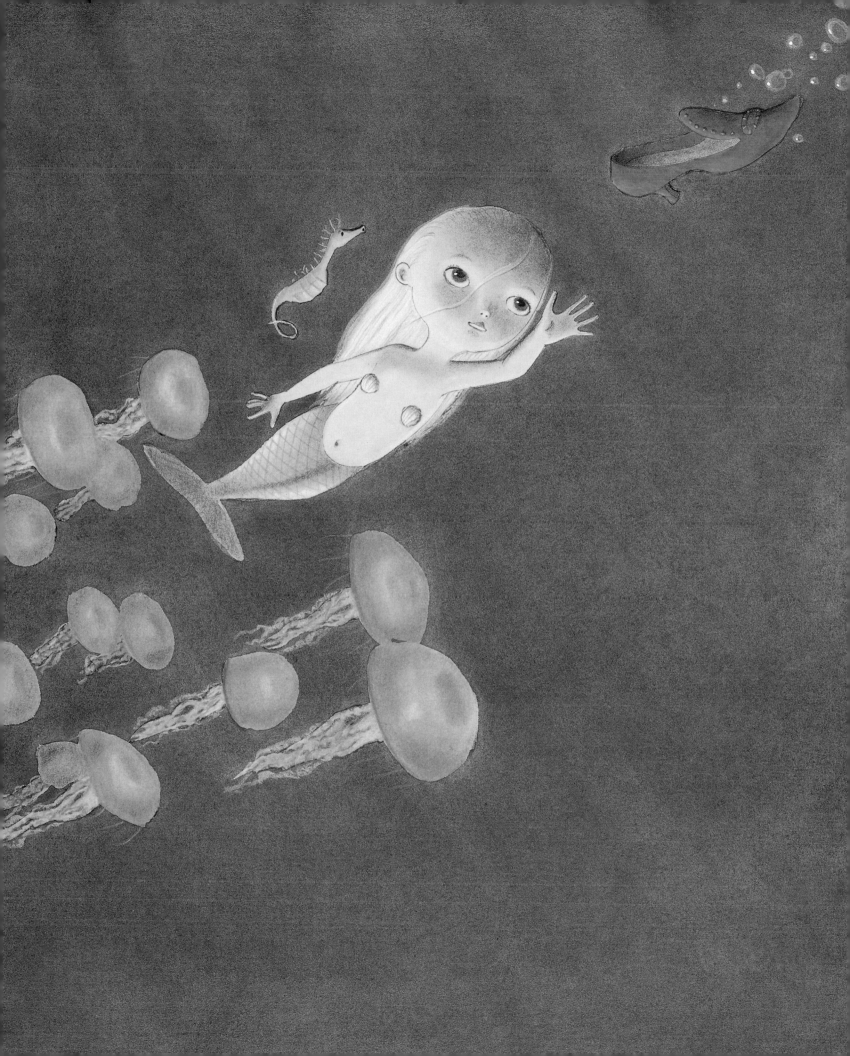

"What is this?" Minnow asked Clio.
"Perhaps," said her sister, "it's a hat."
But the thing was a poor fit,
and not at all flattering.

"What is this?" she asked Thetis.
"Perhaps," said her sister,
"it's a jewel box."
But the thing was wobbly
and spilled pearls all
over Minnow's grotto.

"What is this?" she asked Calypso.

"Questions, questions!" snapped her sister. "It's junk. Useless. Like you."

"This thing," insisted Minnow, "was made with care.

It has a purpose, and I will discover it!"

So off she set, into the warm current,

from whence the thing had come.

In the forest, she passed an octopus.
"What is this?" she asked it.
But the octopus just shrugged.

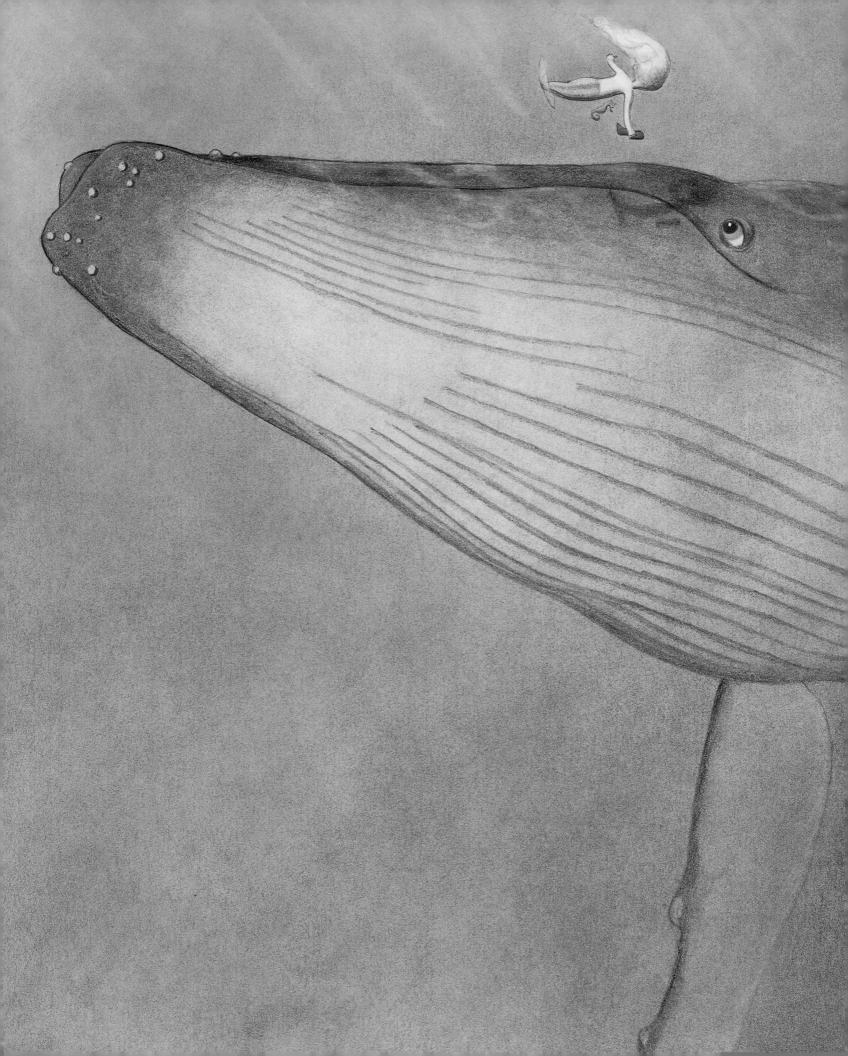

In the shallows, she happened upon a whale.
"What is this?" she asked it.
"I swallowed one of those once,"
said the whale. "Yuck!"

Near the surface, she passed some crabs.
"What is this?" she asked them.
"Don't eat us!" shrieked the startled crabs,
scuttling onto the rocky shore.
"Aha!" thought Minnow (who wasn't even hungry).
"*That's* why they don't have fins."
But she was running out of creatures to question.

She had arrived at the edge of the kingdom,
where bubbles burst and the above place began.
"What a wondrous world!" gasped Minnow,
eyes wide as sand dollars.
Overhead were curious fish that made an awful
racket. The coral was dull like seaweed, and the
seaweed was brilliant like coral. Nearby stood a huge
shell with a door. But there was nothing like the
lovely thing. And no one to tell her what it was
for. Minnow could journey no farther.
Disappointed, she turned to leave.
"I'm afraid," she told the thing,
"we are useless after all."

Suddenly, an odd creature burst from the shell.
It was half mermaid, but with two octopus legs.
And on those legs … was a pair of the lovely things.

"Don't get your shoes wet!"
yelled a voice from the door.

So the landmaid removed them, and Minnow finally
knew *exactly* what the lovely things were for.
Concealed within was another set of ... *hands*.

"But so ugly," she gasped.
"So knobby and gnarled. And *smelly!*"

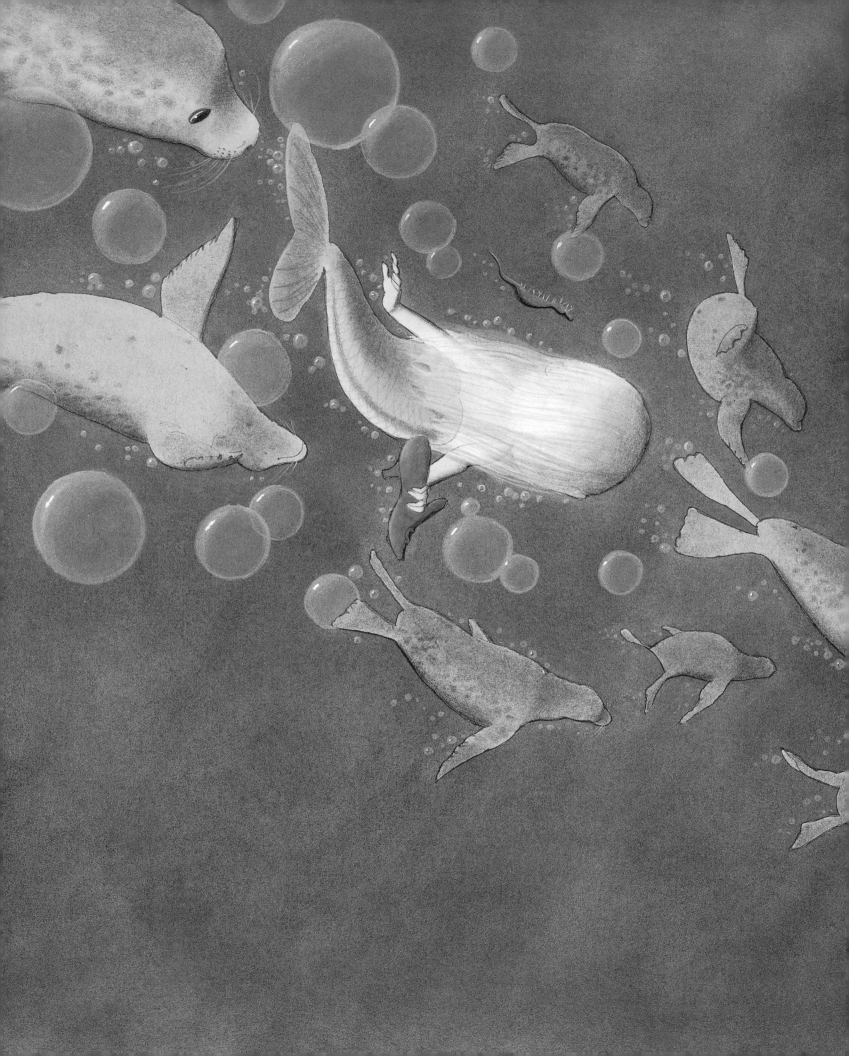

Bursting with news, Minnow returned home
as fast as her tail could carry her.

Excitedly, she urged the entire
court to gather round to listen.

She told them why crabs don't have fins.
She told them of the place beyond
the kingdom, where the bubbles went.
She told them of the noisy fish and
giant shell homes. She told them of the
landmaid and of shoes and the monstrous
leg-hands they were made to hide.

When she was done, Calypso rolled her eyes.
"What," she scoffed, "a *useless* story!"

But King Neptune beamed and hugged his smallest child.
"My Minnow," he boasted to the entire kingdom, "is a daring *explorer*!"

And everyone (except Calypso) clapped
their hands, fins and tentacles in agreement.
"Will you tell us more?" they cried.

"That," said Minnow, "is what I'm here for!"

And she recounted her adventures until
the starfish came out and the anemones fell asleep.